How the Sun Was Brought Back to the Sky

Adapted from a Slovenian Folk Tale

By Mirra Ginsburg

Pictures by Jose Aruego and Ariane Dewey

 A Children's Choice® Book Club Edition From Scholastic Inc.

Macmillan Publishing Co., Inc.
New York

Macmillan Publishing Co., Inc., 866 Third Avenue, New York, N.Y. 10022
Printed in the United States of America
ISBN 0-590-75782-2

For Masha — M. G.

One day gray clouds, huge as mountains, covered the sky. They stayed on, and on, and on. And the sun did not come out for three whole days.

The chicks got worried. It was cold and sad without sunshine. "Where could the sun have gone?" they cried. "We'll go and bring it back into the sky!"

"How will you find it?" clucked the mother hen. "Do you know where it lives?"

"We don't know where it lives," the chicks said, "but we shall ask the way of anyone we meet."

The mother hen prepared the chicks for the long journey. She gave each one a grain of rye and a poppy seed.

The chicks set out. They walked and walked, until they reached a vegetable patch. In the middle of it was a huge head of cabbage, and on the bottom leaf sat a snail. He was large, with big horns, and he carried his house on his back.

"Snail, snail," the chicks asked, "can you tell us where the sun lives?"

"I don't know. Ask the magpie, over on the fence. She might tell you."

The busy magpie did not wait for the chicks to come to her. She flew down to them, chattering, clattering with her beak:

"Chicks, chicks, where are you going? Where are you going, chicks, chicks?"

"The sun has not come out for three days. We're going to look for it."

"I'll come with you, I'll come with you!"

"Do you know where the sun lives?"

"I don't, but the rabbit may know. His home is in the furrow right behind the cabbage patch," the magpie said. "I'll take you there."

The rabbit saw that guests were coming. He wiped his whiskers
with his paw and opened his gate as wide as it would go.

"Rabbit, rabbit," the chicks peeped, the magpie chattered. "We are
looking for the sun. Do you know where it lives?"

"Well, I don't, but my neighbor, the duck, may know. Her home is
in the reeds, by the brook."

The rabbit led them to the brook. The duck's house stood right by the water, and a boat was tied up nearby.

"Are you home, neighbor?" cried the rabbit.

"I'm home, home," quacked the duck. "The sun's been gone for three days now. I can't dry out."

"Well, we're looking for the sun," cried the chicks, the magpie, and the rabbit. "Do you know where it lives?"

"I don't. But there's a tree across the brook. The hedgehog's home is in the hollow among the roots. He's sure to know, he knows everything."

They got into the boat and crossed the brook. The hedgehog lay
rolled up, dozing under the tree.

"Hedgehog, hedgehog," cried the chicks, the magpie, the rabbit, and
the duck. "Do you know where the sun lives? It hasn't been out in
the sky for three days. Maybe it is sick."

The hedgehog thought a while and said:

"Of course, I know where it lives. Behind my tree there is a mountain.
On top of the mountain there's a cloud. Over the cloud lives the
silver moon. And from the moon to the sun it's only a short walk."
The hedgehog took a stick and walked ahead to show
everybody else the way.

They climbed to the top of the mountain where the cloud was resting. The chicks, the magpie, the rabbit, the duck, and the hedgehog got up on the cloud. They sat down comfortably to make sure they wouldn't fall off, and the cloud flew with them straight to the moon's house.

The moon saw them coming and quickly lit its silver horns.
"Moon, moon," cried the chicks, the magpie, the rabbit, the duck,
and the hedgehog. "Show us where the sun lives! It hasn't come out
for three days, and everything is sad and cold without it."

The moon brought them directly to the sun's house. The windows were dark, there was no light anywhere. The sun, they thought, must be asleep and didn't want to wake.

The magpie chattered loudly, the chicks peeped, the duck quacked, the rabbit flapped his ears, and the hedgehog banged his stick on the door.

"Sun, sun, world's delight, come out, give us warmth and light!"

"Who is that shouting under my window?" grumbled the sun. "Who isn't letting me sleep?"

"Your friends — the chicks, the magpie, the rabbit, the duck, and the hedgehog. We've come to wake you. It's time to get up!"

"Oh, oh!" groaned the sun. "How can I show myself now? For three long days, gray clouds shut me out of the sky. I don't even know how to shine any more."

The rabbit heard this and he ran down to the well and brought a pail of water. The duck began to wash the sun. The magpie dried it with a towel. The hedgehog polished it with his bristles. And the chicks picked every speck of dust off its face.

The sun looked out of the sky, clean, fresh, and golden, spreading light and warmth everywhere. And all the animals slid down its rays back to their homes.

The mother hen came out into the sunshine. "Cluck, cluck," she called to her chicks. They gathered around her, running here and there, looking for crumbs and seeds, as bright and gay and golden as the sun itself.

And if you don't believe my story, look out of the window
and you'll see: the hen is there, the chicks are there, and the sun is there,
and doesn't that prove that every word I said is true?